② A STORMGATE PRESS

NIGHT VISION

CHARLES F. MILLHOUSE

I

STORMGATE PRESS

stormgatepress.com
stormgatepress@gmail.com

First Printing: 2024
ISBN: 9798325247811
Imprint: Independently published

Introducing the Stormgate Press Quick Read Books

Short Story Pulp Adventure Books reminiscent of the dime store novels of old.

BOOK 1: The Purple Mystique

BOOK 2: Night Vision

BOOK 3: A Zane Carrington Adventure

Watch for more books in the series coming soon...

Plunge into a whirlpool of action with Zane Carrington: the reckless soldier of fortune and misfortune....... on the high seas to adventure!

There was on average sixty-two crimes a day in New York City in 1938, according to the district attorney's office almost six-hundred and thirty in a week. Of those, there were eighteen murders. Statistics that go unnoticed by the city's unsuspecting population, until their lives become just another number in the ever-growing list of victims.

MURDER AFTER MIDNIGHT

PART I

Darkness surrounded her, fear entangled her, and she ran, she ran as if her life depended on it, because it did. Her heart pounded in her chest like a sledgehammer – her legs weighed heavy as if chained to cinderblocks and her eyes were blinded by tears. Death loomed over her, as certain as if she knew her own name – but she ran anyway.

Darting through Central Park, she hoped the well-lit sidewalks would give her an advantage. She slowed her pace, keeping a cautious eye behind her, certain her pursuer would emerge at any moment.

She brushed a strand of her blond hair out of her waterlogged eyes and stilled her nerves. A streetlight engulfed her and for a moment she thought herself safe.

She was a lovely woman, in her mid-twenties, her classic features reminiscent of a silent movie star, slim and elegant. Her skin was unnaturally light, as if she hadn't spent a lot of time in the sun. She wore a gray-blue dress, with a black collar, and a thin strand of pearls. She clutched a small handbag in her left hand. Her feet were bare, except for her dark silk stockings, her high heal shoes abandoned several blocks back for better mobility.

A trash can toppled in the distance, and she spun around on the balls of her feet. The shrill of a cat, drew her attention – then it appeared out of the dark. A black mass of *something*. It was too bulky to be a man – it was something more – purely evil.

The woman stumbled backward, her feet slipped out from under her and she fell to the concrete sidewalk with a thud; her handbag flung from her grip. A sharp pain cut through her body, but she didn't cry out or make any sound.

Scrambling to her feet she did not run. The black mass filled her vision – she focused on it, prepare to meet death on her terms.

When the unwavering mass moved closer toward its victim, its bulky form transformed into another shape. Less cumbersome, yet just as evil. The linear form slithered ahead and struck as fiercely as a snake. The woman gasped when the blade of a knife sliced into her midsection, the look of astonishment twisted her features and a single tear streamed down her cheek. She slid off the blade and folded to the sidewalk with a gruesome thud.

The dark mass of evil stood there, studying its victim as an artist would a sculpture, proud of its work.

Suddenly the black mass turned, its sharp silver eyes seething with hate, and hissed, "*I see you...*"

Simon Rook came out of the vision in a cold sweat, coming to his feet he steadied himself with the edge of his large mahogany desk, unable to get the piercing cold stare of the killer out of his mind. His visions had always been intense, ripping away a part of his soul. In the years since his visions began, none of them ever communicated with him. It was as if the killer knew he was there. *That's not possible*, he thought. He rubbed his eyes and brought them into focus. He stood in his dimly lit room, trying to get his heartbeat under control and shake off the foreboding feeling that came with this vision.

Simon's visions had been a part of his life since he was sixteen. It wasn't until his early twenties that he understood what the visions were. Murders, and crimes that would happen that night. He tried to tell the police, but they laughed at his warnings not taking him seriously. He could not allow harm to come to these people, so he decided to take matters in his own hands.

If the people who knew him, knew how he spent his nights, dressed in a mask and hood protecting the innocent, he might find himself in a Psychiatric Ward somewhere. Simon understood the risks, but he was compelled to help. He considered it more help than he received growing up with an abusive father.

"Professor, Professor Rook," a knock came to his office door. "Are you alright, Sir?"

Simon steeled his nerves, and said, "Yes Lori, I'm alright, you can come in."

Lori Gail was a slender middle-aged woman with shoulder length corn silk hair and big round cobalt eyes. She came to work for Simon at the beginning of his tenure at the university, and he came to relied on her. Lori watched out for him in a motherly fashion, and that's how Simon looked on her. Sort of a mother and a wife rolled into one.

"I heard you call out. Are you sure you're alright? You're as white as a sheet."

Simon put a hand up, and replied, "Yes, yes, I'm fine. I had a bad dream is all."

"You were sleeping? You have class in ten minutes."

Simon focused on his wristwatch, and scooped up his tweed jacket off the back of his desk chair and said, "You have the list of students?"

Lori pointed at the large desk and said, "I put it there last night, don't you remember?"

"Yes, of course. I was out late last night and forgot to take it home with me."

"You're out late every night. You need to slow down a little. It's dangerous out there, what with sightings of that ghost."

Simon blinked a couple times, and asked, "Ghost?"

"He's all over the news on the radio and in the papers. It gives me the willies."

Simon smiled. Seems his appearances in the city hadn't gone unnoticed as he hoped. His missions into the night to fight for those in danger were not for accolades. He simply wanted to help.

"Here, you'll need these," Lori said picking up a pair of prescription sunglasses and handed them over.

Simon hitched a smile and put on the special lenses. He suffered from a unique form of day blindness. Bright lights rendered him blind, an abnormality brought about from his father's constant physical abuse and strikes to Simon's head. Though there hadn't been a reason for it, Simon was sure the beatings he received from his father also brought about his visions. Visions of crimes that would happen that night.

He picked up his attaché case and a walking cane and brazened out of his office as Lori reminded him, "You have a meeting this afternoon at three o'clock. Try and remember."

"Have I ever been late for a meeting?" Simon asked.

"All the time," Lori said as the office door closed behind him.

Simon walked outside onto the campus of New York University, where he had been teaching economics since nineteen thirty-five. With four years behind him, he strived to mix his teaching with his increasing night life. No matter how hard he tried, he was compelled to go out each night in an attempt to stop the crimes from his visions, each ending in various different degrees of success.

His visions always came during the day and without warning. They came on quickly and ended the same way – leaving him cold and distant as if he lost a piece of his soul.

The death of the woman from his vision today, was now a part of him. He could no more forget her face, than he could his own.

Some visions were simple muggings, or break ins. Then there were the ones like today. Brutal murders, and attacks. If he was lucky, on most days he would receive one vision, but on rare occasions he would have multiple premonitions, and like some sick game, he had to determine which were the more important. Who would he save, and who would he not?

As per his contract, Simon's classroom faced away from the mid-morning sun, and all of his classes were scheduled to finish before mid-afternoon, with the occasional evening classes.

"Good morning," Simon said upon entering the class. He strolled past the first row of desks and went to the windows pulling down the blinds, darkening the room. The students were aware of his handicap on enrolling, and no one complained about the dim light in which to work.

His desk at the front of the room was not as ornate or lovely as his large mahogany, but it was sufficient. He placed his briefcase atop it, and pulled out his list of student names, and began to match the names to the faces in his room. He stopped when he came to an empty seat, third row back. "Seems we have someone tardy," he said. "Does anyone know a Miss Natalie Green?"

No one replied, and Simon continued to go through his list of names, finding the remainder of the class in attendance.

"Alright, if everyone will take out your notebooks, we will begin the spring semester by talking about businessmen of the twentieth century, starting with the success of Captain Steven Hawklin and his impending trial in Crown City and how that will affect his notoriety and..."

The classroom door opened, and all eyes turned toward the lovely woman coming into the room. She was of mid-height and wore a gray-blue dress, with a black collar, that cut off just below the knees – dark silk stockings ran the remainder of her legs.

"I'm sorry I'm late Professor," she said in a silky tone. "I got turned around on campus."

Simon drew a breath to reply but held it when the woman's face came into view. It was the woman from his vision, right down to the strand of pearls around her neck. It took him off guard. He'd never come face to face unexpectedly with a victim from his visions beforehand. He studied her, having only seen her in the clouded mist of his mind. She was even lovelier in person. Her soft white milky skin and subtle hazel eyes were simple, yet pleasant to look at.

Someone coughed, and Simon realized everyone in the room was looking at him. He cleared his throat, and said, "That's quite alright, Miss Green. Please don't make a habit of it. Take your seat."

After a long lecture, and conversation that distracted Simon, the bell rang, and the students poured out of the room in a rush, as Simon reminded them, "Have a ten-page summary of Steven Hawklin's strengths and weaknesses on my desk by Friday morning, and make sure to include a program model of how he should diversify moving into the new decade, and how his trial will affect him."

As Simon gathered his things, shoving papers and notes into his briefcase, he glanced a shadowed movement. "Miss Green," he said seeing the young woman lingering near the desk. "Is there something I can help you with?"

"No Professor," she said in a soft tone. "I just wanted to thank you for understanding my tardiness."

"As long as you don't make a habit out of it, we won't say any more about it," Simon said refraining from saying anything more. Unsure what prolong contact with a victim would do to the outcome tonight. His visions came and went without warning, and he filed them in categories, from least important, like break-ins and vandalisms, to most important, like attacks and murder. Natalie Green was in the most important category – having seen what very well could be her death. The last thing Simon needed was to become too attached to her. *That's the problem*, he thought. *I already am.*

Natalie offered a worrisome smile and continued to loiter. Her soft expression hardened, and she kept her fingers to her mouth, chewing on them nervously.

With his personal affects gathered, Simon stopped short of the door and turned. His inaction, or lack of concern for Natalie's apprehension might be a factor. *If I say or do nothing....* He drew a breath, and said, "Is everything alright Miss Green?"

"You might think I'm silly, Professor, but I've had this peculiar feeling that I've been followed all day. I was late to class because I was trying to make sure I wasn't being followed."

"And where you?" Simon asked.

Natalie hitched a smile, and said, "I don't know."

Again, Simon wasn't sure how to react. He could do the simplest thing and offer her a ride home, wherein she wouldn't encounter that thing in the park, but Simon wasn't sure what would happen. If he changed his vision, he would be changing the future and he'd never done that before. *What would be the implications?* he wondered.

"Can you call someone?" he asked.

Again, Natalie offered a worrisome smile. "There's no one to call," she said.

"I see, well..."

"It's alright Professor. I'm just being a nervous nelly. I'll be alright."

Against his better judgement, and even after telling himself not to, Simon said, "Let me offer you a ride home at least."

Natalie's expression brightened a bit, but quickly dulled, and she said, "Thank you, but no Professor, that wouldn't be proper."

Simon swallowed, and drew a hesitant breath, and said, "No. Perhaps you're right." All the while wishing he could do or say something to prevent her inevitable future. This was an opportunity never offered him before. Even with his prescient abilities it seemed he couldn't change things to come. He always thought his visions were a gift, and in many ways they were. Yet at that moment he realized they were also a curse.

The next class began to amble into the room. Simon looked at the time and remembered his scheduled meeting. He focused, as Natalie shuffled her way out of the room amid the arriving students.

Simon gathered his belongings, and chased after her, only to lose her in the flow of people in the corridor. He paused, bumping into a student or two, who apologized as Simon brushed past them, swimming upstream in an attempt to get out of the building.

Outside, the quad bustled with activity, and the bright morning sun shocked Simon's senses, as he dug his special sunglasses out of his pocket and shoved them on his face. Despite the protective lenses, the bright glow washed his vision, and even though he saw the mass of people in front of him, their forms were sluiced, their features masked. *I've lost her...*

"There you are Professor," Lori said when Simon entered his office. "Your appointment has been waiting."

"Cancel it," Simon replied.

"But he's already in your office," Lori said. "I sat him in there with a cup of coffee nearly twenty minutes ago."

Simon stepped further into the outer office, and said, "Call Atticus and have him pick me up please."

"But your meeting," Lori huffed.

Simon released a breath, "Alright, I'll see him. But please call Atticus."

Lori scooped up the phone receiver in her hand, as Simon stepped into his office and closed the door. His vision equalized in the dim light, and he glimpsed a form sitting in the chair near his large desk.

"My apologies," Simon said. "It's a bit of a hectic day."

"That's quite alright Professor Rook," the man said in a thick New Hampshire accent. He stood and turned toward Simon, holding an oversized portfolio in his right hand. "This interview won't last long."

Simon crossed to the other side of his desk eyeing the tall stocky man. "I'm afraid I haven't been briefed about this meeting mister...?"

"Payne. Morgan Payne."

"Mister Payne," Simon said motioning for Morgan to sit, as he lowered himself into his desk chair. "Why are you here exactly?"

Morgan Payne reclined in his chair and regarded Simon for a moment. Payne's long narrow features were stolid, regal, and menacing. "The university is conducting a research study on its faculty, and I'm afraid it's your turn," he said with a dark smile.

"What kind of research?" Simon inquired skeptically. He wasn't aware of any interdepartmental research study.

"Nothing too intense," Morgan replied. "They want to know a bit more about who teaches at the university. To better evaluate just who you are."

"So, this is a psychiatric evaluation?"

"Of sorts, you understand."

Simon sat forward, and with his hands flat on the desk, said, "No, I'm afraid I don't. This feels like an invasion of privacy."

Forgoing more preamble, Morgan opened his portfolio, skimmed his long index finger down a page and said, "You were orphaned."

"No," Simon replied. "My mother died when I was young. *My* father was charged and sentenced with her death. He's been sitting on death row ever since. *I* really don't see what this has to do with my teaching ability."

"You are resentful."

"I'm sorry was that a question or a statement?" Simon asked.

"For the death of your mother," Payne pressed.

With tension in the air, Simon held a tight breath in his chest, and said, "My father is a loathsome man, with nothing but hatred in him. He hated me, and to tell the truth I'm not sure he ever loved my mother."

"How does that..."

Simon went to his feet and he fisted the top of the desk. "My father would beat me, slap me around every chance he got. My mother would take the brunt of my beatings herself, to spare me. By doing so, it drove her to her grave, and left me with this damnable day blindness because I took one too many hits to the head. If my father had his wish, I'd be in a plot next to my mom, and he wouldn't be sorry for either of our deaths."

"Yes, but how does that make you..."

"I hate him, Mister Payne. Is that what you want to hear me say? Well, I'll say it again. I hate him. This interview is over, good afternoon, *Sir*." Simon rounded the desk, and held the office door open, waiting for Payne to stand.

"You have a hatred in your heart too, don't you Mister Rook?"

"The only hate I have is because I have to suffer through an interrogation such as this, and I... I..."

Payne stood slowly from his chair, his hands shimmered a bright orange, and he said, "Is there something a matter, Mister Rook?"

The vision came on without warning, like they always did. Simon found himself transported through space and time. Night loomed upon him like a blanket of pure evil, as images tunneled around him. To be transported yet again, to witness another crime was unbelievable, yet there he was staring at the victim of a brutal beating only inches from him. The body was mulled – not an inch of the corpse was untouched. The victim was a woman and for a handful of heartbeats Simon thought it might be Natalie, but the body configuration didn't match his student's slender form. Her face unrecognizable, her clothes drenched in dark amber, the odor of copper lingered on the air.

The heinous crime looked more like an animal attack than something done by another human. Then Simon saw them, footprints in the blood, and beyond that the image of... something. He squinted to get a better look, but the form was nimble, and masked itself in the shadows.

"*I see you,*" the insidious voice growled, and Simon screamed.

PART II

Simon came out of the vision gasping for breath.

"Professor, Professor," Lori called. "Are you alright?"

Simon took inventory of his surroundings before regarding Lori. He drew his tongue over his lips, feigned ignorance and said, "What happened?"

"I was about to ask you the same thing," Lori replied. She was his personal secretary. Privy to many aspects of his life at the university, though Lori knew nothing of his visions. That secret was closely guarded.

Simon cleared his vision, scoured the room, and asked, "Where is Mister Payne?"

"He took out of here in a rush," Lori said. "He didn't say a word."

Simon stepped back into his office, glimpsed the clock on the wall, and turned. "Has Atticus arrived?"

"He's out front, waiting," Lori said, and questioned, "Are you alright. You gave me a start."

"It's just been a long day. Too much of the sun, I suspect," Simon said, hoping his lie wasn't prevalent.

Lori's brow tightened, but she didn't reply. Simon could tell by her wan expression she didn't believe him.

Scooping up his jacket, Lori helped Simon slip his arms into the coat without a word, as he fisted his briefcase and headed toward the door.

"Professor."

Simon turned back and offered Lori a congenial smile.

"Try and get some rest," she said.

Simon replied with a nod, before exiting the office.

It was still high sun when Simon slid into the backseat of the Chevrolet Master Deluxe sedan with special blackened windows. Atticus Harper sat behind the steering wheel. "Where to?" he asked.

"The Tower," Simon said. "Be discrete."

"Aren't I always?" he asked. Atticus Harper was a brawny man in his late thirties with a thick black beard, that partially hid an aged knife scar that came across his right eye and trailed down to the bend of his neck. He wore a bracelet on his left hand. The all-seeing eye. Over the years many others join Night Vision's Watchmen, but Atticus was the first.

Simon met Atticus while in college, having saved him from death at the hands of a mob boss on the east side of Chicago. His vision of Atticus' murder was one of the first he ever thwarted. He found a friend in Atticus who repaid him by becoming Simon's private chauffeur, though at the time Simon could barely buy food, but Atticus considered it repayment for his life.

"You seem troubled."

Simon pinched the bridge of his nose with his thumb and index finger. "I had a second vision today," he said.

15

Atticus' eyes furrowed in the rearview mirror and he said, "A second... that doesn't happen a lot."

"There's something else," Simon said in a wrenched tone.

Atticus glanced at the road, and then back to Simon without a word.

"The body in the second vision was already dead. In all my visions, the victim has always been alive, with the action of the crime part of the prophecy."

"What's it mean?"

Simon recounted his predictions, making sure to tell his friend of the first victim, *his* student, and his strange encounter with something lurking in both of his visions.

"It communicated with you?" Atticus asked.

"It was watching me, but I don't know who it was."

Atticus held his breath and returned his eyes to the road in front of the car.

In the six years since he and Atticus decided to do something about his visions, nothing ever happened remotely like this. There were strange cases. Devilish, heinous crimes committed by normal everyday people, but nothing on this scale. It was almost as if, all the cases, the people they saved over the years were nothing but a warmup for something grander, and more aligned with Simon's powers.

Am I ready for this? Simon wondered. *Is Night Vision ready for this?*

Night Vision grew out of desperation. On one hand Simon wanted to stop the crimes his visions presented him, but in turn he wanted to have some kind of normal life. The

16

idea of the mask still seemed silly. What grown man would hide his face to
deal out justice? Every time he pulled the cowl over his head, Simon wondered if it would be the last time. If he were to die wearing the hood and mask, how would his acquaintances deal with the fact that he was a masked vigilante? Would they even care? His only true friend was Atticus, and Simon believed that whatever happened to him, Atticus would share in that fate.

The sedan pulled up to an abandoned fire station on Manhattan's east side. The hulking Behemoth of a building sat unused for nearly a decade. In the center of the large structure was a massive tower – the original bell still hung in the top of the construct and Simon spent many of his nights staring out at the city before he went off to prevent whatever his visions showed him. In many ways he was more at home in the firetrap, than at his actual home.

Atticus drove the car through an oversized door, once reserved for the old horse drawn firewagons, and turned off the engine and checked his wristwatch. "It's still several hours before sunset. You have any idea what you're going to do?"

Simon slipped out of the backseat and came around the front of the car. Atticus climbed out of the car and watched Simon but didn't say anything else.

Simon stopped and turned to Atticus. "I go with my initial vision. I know where Natalie will be and what time."

"And what of the other victim?"

Simon rubbed his face and put his hand to the back of his neck. "I don't even know who she is, or where she was in my second vision. Even if I wanted to prevent her death, my vision didn't show me anything concrete."

"Maybe we should call the police."

"And tell them what?"

Atticus winced. "I get your point."

"We go after Natalie. It's all we can do."

"And what if it isn't?" Atticus asked. "We've never faced anything like this before."

Simon didn't have an answer and he wished he did. Ascending the staircase into the tower, he fought with memories long since buried. Memories brought back to him after the visit by Morgan Payne. Simon lived with constant agony, both physical and mental at the hands of his destructive father. Ice chilled Simon's blood as he fought the painful memories.

"We do what we always do," Simon said. "We protect those who can't protect themselves."

"But if someone is going to die..."

Simon thought a moment, and said, "How many murders happen in this town in a week? In all those deaths we are shown maybe one, or two. People die, Atticus we can't stop them all. We're going to fail someone tonight, but we will save someone too."

***

The idea of Night Vision came out of a need to save people. The mask and hood were to give Simon a sense of normalcy, though Simon's life was anything but normal. In the weeks after his decision to become a barb of justice, Simon took his licks. In many cases his sense of duty led to many failures, having taken the brunt of the battle – being beaten near death many times, he refused to give up. He refused to allow one person to die, and in the six years the crimes Simon thwarted, all ended with him as victor, and the murders he'd envisioned, ended with the people being saved.

In six years, his fighting skills improved, even though his impediment was a hindrance, he took precautions, fitting his mask with special light reflecting lenses, that prevented bright lights from blinding him. He carried a Browning Auto-Five shotgun for those times when accuracy wasn't possible and he wore a utility belt filled with extra ammunition, smoke bombs and garrote wire.

"Are you ready?" Atticus asked when he stepped into the weapons room.

Simon turned, dressed in his protective grey suit, he snapped his belt in place. "Ready," he said.

Atticus stood quiet for a minute. His face tight with apprehension.

"You have something to say?" Simon asked.

"I've got this funny feeling about tonight is all."

Simon didn't reply with words of reassurance, the thought of easing Atticus would do nothing for his own self-doubt. The idea that tonight could be the end, never crossed his mind, but it loomed over him as an inevitability. "We do this by the book," he said.

Atticus nodded, though it seemed like he wanted to say something, he didn't.

"You drop me off on the north end of the park and pick me up on the south end."

"It's what happens between point A and point B that has me worried."

"You're never a nervous nelly," Simon said with a smirk.

Atticus laughed, and shook his head in response, even with a cloud of gloom in the air.

The drive from the tower went in silence. Simon sat in the backseat, hunkered in the dark to mask his presence from others. Atticus never once looked back at him in the rearview mirror, but Simon watched his friend's eyes when a streetlight or passing car highlighted them. They were full of worry and desperation. For a passing moment, Simon considered turning around, and allow things to playout normally – he thought otherwise. Living with that decision would haunt him for the rest of his life. However the cards fell this night, he would face them eyes forward, and ready.

"See you soon," was all Atticus said when Simon stepped out of the car as Night Vision, replied, "Soon."

Night Vision took to the shadows of the park, keeping off the beaten path so park strollers wouldn't see him. The trollop of a horse and buggy crossing along the thoroughfare filled the night and the sound of an accordion and applause came from a tiny cropping of people in a small clearing.

This isn't where it happened, Night Vision thought and he moved further away from the populated areas. He'd recognize where the attack would happen when he saw it.

Deeper into the park he traveled, and soon he was alone. That's when it came upon him. A sense of cold filled the air. The spring night quickly turned bitter, which wasn't unusual in New York, but this kind of cold bit at him, seeping into his skin and chilled his bone. The presence of another being stirred somewhere nearby and Night Vision hunkered in the bushes, watching, waiting.

Moments later, the sound of footfalls filled the night and he peered over the bushes to find Natalie Green, just like it was in his vision. Scared, confused, and running for her life.

Night Vision fought the urge to spring from his hiding spot even though every passing moment brought his student closer to death, but he waited for the perpetrator to show himself.

The air became colder, and Night Vision's hands trembled as he held onto his Browning. Preparing to spring from his spot, Night Vision froze, when a black-clad form came out of the night. Natalie stumbled backward, losing her footing she fell back onto the concrete sidewalk and screamed.

Night Vision broke cover – his finger tightened on the trigger of his shotgun, but he hesitated, narrowing his sights down the barrel of his gun. "Stand to," he ordered, but the black form didn't move. "I said, stand to."

Without warning, the form turned holding something in his hand, instantly Night Vision's sight blurred and he dropped his shotgun to the pavement, it made a clatter on impact.

With the crook of his right arm over his eyes, and his left hand shoved in front of him in a vain attempt to push back the blinding light, Night Vision dropped to his knees. The cackle of his attacker filled the night, and then a sharp dazzling light came to the back of Night Vision's eyes, and he toppled to the ground in a pool of black.

PART III

The flash of dim light sent a piercing hard stab into the back of Night Vision's head when he opened his eyes. Sharp pricks of needles burned his arms when he woke – they held the brunt of his weight as he dangled from a support beam above. He surveyed his surroundings, bright light washed his vision, but he managed to make out the form of Natalie Green crumpled on the floor near him. Motionless, he feared the worse until he saw the slight heaving of her chest moving up and down. She was breathing, *she's alive,* he thought.

Shifting his body, Night Vision managed to put his weight on his legs, as he found his footing and stood. The rope was taught, and it sliced into his flesh cutting off the circulation. *Just a flick of the wrist,* he thought trying to activate the spring in his gauntlet and produce the hidden blade within. *Come on, come on. Damn it.*

"You're awake," a voice from the shadows called out.

Night Vision didn't respond. Instead, he scoured the area where the voice came.

"I didn't think you would be that easy to bring down," the faceless voice said. "Evidently I was wrong."

Night Vision tightened the muscles in his arms and leaned toward the voice, the voice he recognized. "Show yourself."

"The papers paint you as some kind of Street level Messiah, and clearly you do have a god complex, otherwise I wouldn't have been able to bring you down so easily. Know thine enemy."

"Am I supposed to be impressed?" Night Vision asked.

"Please," the voice said. "Don't act as if you don't know who I am." The form manifested from the shadows, and Morgan Payne came into view.

"You don't seem surprised," Payne said.

"Should I be?"

"Considering I was in your office this afternoon. You should be a bit more shocked that I'm here... yes."

Damn it, Night Vision grimaced. *He knows who I am. Or does he?*

"Your silence won't deter me, Mister Rook. You see, I've been watching you for several weeks. I've invaded your visions on more than one occasion, and I was there when you saw young Miss Green run for her life. Everything is by design. Her fate was to be nothing but a lure, and it worked just as I foresaw."

"Who are you?"

"I am who I claimed to be. I am Morgan Payne, my job is to analyze, study and report."

"To whom?"

"That doesn't concern you. Not yet," Payne replied. "All you need to know right now, is that you will know pain, you will know suffering, and then you will know death."

24

"By your hands?" Night Vision asked.

Payne gave an insidious toothy grin, and said, "Not by me..."

"Who then?"

Payne's face slacked, emotionless and he said, "When we last met, you spoke of your father. How did that make you feel?"

Night Vision stilled his tongue.

"You must answer me," Payne said.

Still, Night Vision didn't reply.

"You have to answer me."

"No, I do not," Night Vision replied, angling his body to align himself with Payne. *Just come a little closer, you bastard... a little closer.*

"You cannot bait me, Mister Rook."

Night Vision relaxed, *no, I guess I won't.* He drew a breath, but before he spoke, Natalie Green stirred on the floor.

Payne turned toward her. "Our guest awakes."

Night Vision lunged forward, applying strength to his bindings and pulling them to their zenith. "Leave her alone...!" he ordered.

Natalie turned, and recoiled when she saw Payne, and Night Vision. "Who are you?" she demanded. The words tight in her throat.

"You are not in danger, my dear," Payne said unconvincingly. "As long as Mister Rook agrees to cooperate."

Natalie's face wrinkled, and asked, "Mister Rook?"

Again, Night Vision relaxed. "State your questions," he said.

Payne wheeled around. His hands aglow, he stalked forward. "Your father," he said flatly. "Your discontent, your torment, your shame."

Night Vision studied Payne as the man stalked forward. There was a familiarity about him, something Night Vision couldn't decipher, yet clearly, he had some kind of power in him that set him apart from the simple run of the mill street thug. "What are you?" he chagrined. "How are you doing this?"

"Think of me as your conscience," Payne moved around Night Vision like a predatory animal. "Your hatred is prevalent. I am here to remind you of it."

"Remind me?"

"You hate him, don't you?"

"Oh, yes," Night Vision admitted. Imagery from his childhood flooded his memories. The beatings, the verbal abuse, the constant belittlement. The anguish at seeing his mother bleeding on the floor at his father's hand. "My father disgusts me...!" he shouted. "He was a vile despicable person, and I hate him. But he does not define me."

"You lie!" Payne shouted. The luminosity around his hands intensified. "He made you. Your visions are because of him. Visions I share, visions I can control."

"Huh..." The vision came to Night Vision, shrouded in the night. *What is happening?* He fought to gain control. Visions never came to him at night, but this one invaded his senses as clear as a summer's day.

Fires burned all around him. The intoxicating heat stifled him, and Night Vision knew the place in an instant. *The old foundry, on Cheshire Avenue.* The effervescent glow cast a myriad of shadows causing movement everywhere. Then he saw her. "Lori?" His secretary lived near the foundry. By the disgruntled look etched on her features, she was frightened, confused and in trouble.

She's the second victim, Night Vision's stomach tightened when the figures of two men stepped out of the orange glow, and Lori spotted them, she backed away in terror.

Night Vision lurched forward, like all his visions, he could not interfere. All he could do, was watch in horror, as she died.

Suddenly, the vision ended, and Night Vision found himself back in the warehouse. Gunshots echoed throughout the building. He narrowed his eyes trying to focus, catching the glimpse of... "Atticus...?"

"Yeah, it's me," Atticus called from his hiding place.

Footfalls echoed throughout the building as armed men ran everywhere.

"Your friend can do nothing to help you," Payne said.

"You're wrong about that," Night Vision replied. "He's a distraction." With a twist of his wrist, the hidden blade slid forth, instantly cutting the rope holding him and Night Vision dropped to the floor.

The shimmering glow around Payne's hands subsided, and he tugged a pistol from inside his coat. He leveled it on Natalie. "Take one step toward me, and I swear to God, I'll kill her," he warned.

Natalie recoiled, staring into the end of the pistol.

More weapons fire echoed inside the building. Hammering footfalls scattered all around them.

"Your friend is going to die," Payne said assuredly.

"You'll find him more difficult to kill than you believe," Night Vision replied slowly taking another step toward Natalie.

"Your faith in your friend is admirable, *and* you're killing this girl with each step."

Night Vision hesitated.

"That's right," Payne said. "There is nothing you can do to stop me."

"Maybe I can't..."

Payne chuckled. An expression of complete control tightened on his face and he said, "You have too much faith in your man. He is no match for my hired men."

Atticus came out of the dark in a quiet fluid motion, positioning himself behind Payne. He drew up the pistol in his hand and cocked the hammer, and said, "I wouldn't say that."

Payne paled, but drew a strong breath and shouted, "Guards...!"

"What guards...?" Atticus snarled. "They're all dead. Drop your pistol."

Unmoving, Payne stood his ground. His pistol hovered over Natalie.

Atticus shifted his footing, and said, "I will not ask again. Drop your weapon."

"You won't have time to kill me before I kill the girl," Payne said. "Are you willing to take that chance?"

Atticus didn't reply.

A lilt of a laugh came to Payne's voice, and he said, "I didn't think so."

With Payne's attention on Atticus, Night Vision slipped his gloved hand down to his side, reaching into a pouch on his belt.

"You only have two choices," Payne said.

"There is a third," Night Vision said tossing the flashbang to the floor – shielding his eyes before it exploded. The instant shock of light brightened the room, and Payne dropped his pistol – his hands went to his eyes. Night Vision rushed him, throwing a punch sending the rogue to the floor.

Atticus placed a foot on Payne's chest, and said, "There's always another option."

Night Vision went to Natalie, bending down to her on the floor. She held a scream in her throat but recoiled.

"It's alright," Night Vision said yanking the mask from his face.

"Mister Rook...?"

"You're safe now. You're safe."

Natalie trembled, her eyes wrenched in their sockets, and she said, "I... I don't understand."

Still poised over Payne, Atticus admitted, "I'm afraid I don't really know what the hell is going on."

"Lori," Rook scattered to his feet, pulling the mask over his face, and heaving Payne off the floor. "Stop your men."

Payne offered a bloody smile," Even if I could stop them, I wouldn't," he said.

Night Vision tossed Payne aside, as Atticus kept his gun trained on him.

"He has Lori. She's in the old foundry. Where's the car?"

"Six blocks away, in the opposite direction," Atticus said.

29

Night Vision glimpsed his shotgun propped up in a corner and retrieved it. "There's no time," he said bolting for the warehouse door.

"The foundry is nine blocks away," Payne roared with laughter, "You'll *Never* make it in time."

Night Vision darted from the building. Payne's last words ringing in his ears. The thought of Lori's death on his mind. He created his secret persona out of the need to do good. Having lived a life of abuse and tragedy, the idea of saving people, fighting those who would do harm and bringing them to justice was his way of putting his father's pain behind him, and honoring his mother by helping those in need, like she protected him against his abusive father all those years ago.

Lori would not die this night, he swore it to himself, no matter if it meant his own death, she would live... *I swear.*

The night grew long as Night Vision came upon the foundry. The immense old factory of rusted metal, and dilapidated infrastructure still produced metal to this day. Perhaps the call to condemn the old behemoth was justified, but the fact it still produced material and kept hundreds of men working was a huge deal in the midst of a great depression.

Huge flames from the stacks at the top of the main building lit up the deep dark sky. A thunderstorm brewed in the distance – streaks of lightning sheeted overhead.

Keeping to the shadows, Night Vision leapt over the large stone wall that encircled the compound. The foundry was at full production, and the facility teamed with activity as men labored to complete the quota, completely oblivious that a woman fought for her life under their very noses.

Night Vision followed what he saw in his mind, using it as a guide as he homed in on Lori – remembering the look in her eyes when he witnessed the vision.

A flash of lightning exposed him for half a heartbeat, his form nothing but an apparition, and he moved quickly and stealthily before anyone could get a better look at him.

Night Vision recognized the outer building from his vision as he approached. The structure leaned slightly and look as if it were ready to collapse. Deep holes filled the walls and pricks of light shot through rusted fissures.

A horrific scream bellowed in the night, masked by the intense drumming sound from the main foundry building. No one would have heard it, even if they were close – yet Night Vision was entuned. His stomach sank. *God, am I too late?* He burst into the shoddy building, his shotgun out in front of him.

His vision washed some, but the light inside the building wasn't overwhelming and his eyesight adjusted with the use of the special lenses in his mask. He scoured the interior, and silently went deeper into the infrastructure stopping when he saw movement behind a stack of ceramic piping. He hesitated, and regarded the movement before continuing, unsure who it was ahead – friend or foe.

When a wiry man came out from behind a stack of crates to Night Vision's right, he turned charging the attacker, stabbing the man with the end of his shotgun. The force of the blunt attack threw the man off guard and he bellied over, long enough for Night Vision to deliver a swift kick across his face, sending the hood to the floor.

Night Vision turned back to the ceramic piping, waiting for another attack. He charged forward and that's when he saw her. Lori came out in the opening. Haggard and disheveled, her blouse was ripped, and she held it, covering herself.

Stunned by Night Vision's appearance she faltered. "The Ghost," she said in a whispered breath.

Another man came out behind her. He carried a long knife and Night Vision called, "Get down."

Without hesitation, Lori did as she was instructed and Night Vision pulled the trigger, splattering the man with shot. The force of the blast shoved him back – little specks of scarlet decorated the piping behind him.

Night Vision snagged Lori by the arm, and she pushed away. "Don't hurt me," she yelled.

"How many more are there?" he asked.

She eyed him for a few long seconds, and replied in a broken tone, "Two more."

Night Vision wheeled around, cocking his shotgun, sending fresh cartridges into the chamber. "Where?" he asked.

"They were here," Lori said, and then asked, "Who are you?"

Masking his voice, Simon said, "I'm no one." He led Lori out of the building into the rain. Intense light flashed across the sky, temporarily blinding him and he stopped.

"It's just some lightning," Lori said.

Night Vision grimaced. *This is where it happened,* he recalled his vision. He pulled Lori close, and waited.

"What are we..." the words stuck in Lori's throat when the two forms charged them. The sheeting rain masked their forms, but Night Vision saw them clearly in the dimming light. He rose his shotgun to fire, but the first man was quick, and he knocked the weapon from Night Vision's hands. The weapon slapped the wet ground. Night Vision blocked the attack, and Lori screamed. He wheeled around, slipping a knife out of his belt, he lobbed it through the air, catching the second attacker in the shoulder and sending him to the ground in pain.

Night Vision recentered his attention on the first man, but he was gone. Lori came in close to him for protection and asked, "Where did he go?"

Night Vision held his answer, waiting for the shoe to drop, but it never did. "Gone," he said. *Can it be that simple?*

Red lights strobed in through the main gate as several patrol cars came in. Night Vision turned to Lori, "You're safe now," he said and stepped away.

"Wait," Lori reached out. "Who are you."

Night Vision couldn't answer. He refused to answer. Too many people learned his secret tonight. The more who knew of his secret would put him, and them in danger. He touched Lori on the shoulder, and she grabbed his hand, holding it tight, she said, "Wait, Ghost..."

Night Vision took her hand in his, aware the police cars were getting closer. Letting go of Lori, he told her, "I'm Night Vision..." and with that he ran into the rainy night.

***

The outer cell door opened, and Simon Rook followed the officer down the corridor into the detention area. Rook kept his eyes to the grimy floor, as they walked past a series of incarcerated individuals who stared intently. Passing through another outer gate, the officer said, "I can only give you five minutes before shift change. My Sergeant will be by soon. You have to be gone before he arrives."

Simon reached out his hand, and the police officer placed his hand inside Rook's. The officer wore the all-seeing eye bracelet on his right wrist. "Thank you, Watchman," he said. "This won't take long."

Morgan Payne sat at the back of his cell and offered a wide grin. "You have them everywhere, don't you?" he asked. "I wonder how they would react if they knew you were their benefactor?"

Simon ignored the statement and asked, "I came to ask… who are you. And how are you able to control my visions?"

Payne placed his hands on his knees and simply said, "You don't think you're the only one in the world with abilities like yours, do you?"

"Are you saying you have visions, also?"

"I used to, until I learned to control them. Though I daresay my abilities came to me from a car accident. Where yours came to you by a more dubious manner. Either way, you and I are alike."

"We are nothing alike," Simon said. "I help people."

"And I help myself," Payne said. "It's a profitable profession. You should try it."

"And you were hired to what, kill me?"

Payne stood and crossed the cell, stopping at the bars. "Oh, God no. I was hired to test you. To see if you could live up to the challenge, and my employer will be most pleased to find that the hate for your father burns inside you. You really hate him, don't you?"

"How would you feel about a man who killed someone you loved. Can you love I wonder?"

Payne took hold of the bars and squeezed tight. "This isn't over. You know that."

"No, I think it is. I have pity for the person who tries to hurt those in my life again."

"Are you threatening me?" Payne asked.

"Take it however you like," Simon replied. "But the truth is I'll be waiting, and I will stop you."

"Oh, for me, this is over," Payne said. "I did the job I was hired to do. Even though I failed, that won't stop him. He's still coming after you. And he doesn't care who gets in his way. He hates you, as much as you hate him."

Simon's heart skipped a beat, and the blood rushed to his feet. He drew a tight breath.

"You asked, who hired me. But you don't need me to answer that, do you?"

Simon forced out, "No."

Payne's lips parted into a wide toothy grin. "Your father sends his regards."

Simon stepped away from the bars, his heart drummed in his chest, and his throat went cottony dry. The man who fathered him, beat him, killed his mother was still very much a part of him, and it seemed that not even prison would stop him from finishing what he started. Either his father would kill him... or *I'll kill him...* Simon thought.

As Simon Rook walked away from Payne, fighting with the revelation that his father was still very much a part of his life, he didn't notice the afternoon paper sitting on the front desk, and the headline that read: `Night Vision: Eyewitness Gives Name to The Ghost.`
FIN-

Night Vision *will* return...

ABOUT THE AUTHOR

Charles F. Millhouse is an Award-Winning Author and Publisher. He published his first book in 1999 and he hasn't looked back. Having written over thirty books in the Pulp/Science Fiction genres. His imagination is boundless. From the 1930's adventures of Captain Hawklin – through the gritty paranormal old west town of New Kingdom – to the far-off future in the Origin Trilogy, Charles breathes life into his characters, brings worlds alive and sends his readers on journeys they won't soon forget.

Charles lives in Southeastern, Ohio with his wife and two sons.

Visit stormgatepress.com for more details.

Printed in Great Britain
by Amazon